STEERED WRONG

IRON & FLAME COZY MYSTERIES, BOOK 4

PATTI BENNING

SUMMER PRESCOTT BOOKS PUBLISHING

Copyright 2024 Summer Prescott Books

All Rights Reserved. No part of this publication nor any of the information herein may be quoted from, nor reproduced, in any form, including but not limited to: printing, scanning, photocopying, or any other printed, digital, or audio formats, without prior express written consent of the copyright holder.

**This book is a work of fiction. Any similarities to persons, living or dead, places of business, or situations past or present, is completely unintentional.

ONE

Lydia Thackery knew something was wrong as soon as she turned the corner. Jude Holloway, her *friend*, never mind what her sister liked to tease her about, was a game warden. He was a man who loved nature, who spent every day keeping the great outdoors safe from people who thought they could take advantage of it.

He was not the sort of person who threw garbage in his yard, yet the muddy grass that was just beginning to show the first shoots of spring green in front of his house was absolutely covered in trash.

Concerned, she pulled into his driveway, glad that most of the ice and snow had melted. Jude's house was on a hill at the edge of the forest, and his driveway's incline was steep. She had first visited a couple of weeks ago, when winter still had its claws out, and getting up the driveway then had not been fun.

Today, all she had to worry about was slowing down for Saffron, his yellow mixed breed dog. She had one floppy ear and one ear that was pricked up, giving her a goofy, friendly look that matched up with her personality perfectly. Lydia put her SUV into park when the dog loped over to her, and managed to get her door open before she jumped up on it. Saffron greeted her with doggy kisses and an exuberant wagging tail, and Lydia returned the favor with the behind-the-ear scratch she knew the dog loved.

"You're such a good girl. Yes, I missed you too. Oof, you're a muddy girl, watch those paws."

When Saffron's excitement overcame her and she darted away to do zoomies around the yard, Lydia took the opportunity to get out of her vehicle and wave to Jude, who was standing next to the flagpole by the corner of his house, a half-full garbage bag in front of him. Two more bags, full and tied off, were sitting by his front stoop.

"What happened?" she asked in lieu of greeting as she walked across the grass toward him.

"I don't know. I woke up to this," he said. "Probably some kids with nothing better to do. I'm almost done cleaning it up; we can head out now if you're in a hurry, but I'd rather finish this first in case the wind picks up. I don't want all this trash to blow into the trees."

"I'll help," she said, stooping to pick up a soggy pizza box. "Are you going to report this?"

"I'll look through the bags later and see if they left any mail or anything else with their name on it behind."

She frowned as she began picking up trash. A friend's yard getting vandalized wasn't what she had expected this Wednesday morning. Jude seemed to be going through a streak of bad luck lately; his truck had refused to start yesterday, and was currently in the shop, which was why she was picking him up instead of meeting him at the park like usual. They didn't always go on a midweek hike, but it had been a while since they were able to go on their normal weekend hikes, and after the icy, frigid winter, the spring weather was irresistible. Even though the temperature was only in the forties, it seemed balmy compared to the sub-twenties temperatures they'd had when winter was in full swing.

"I think that's the last of it," he said a few minutes later, surveying the yard before tying the last garbage bag shut. "Thanks for helping, it would have taken me twice as long without you."

"You should have let me know what happened earlier, and I would have come to help sooner," she said. "It can't have been fun to spend your morning doing that."

He whistled, calling Saffron over from where she was investigating the tires on Lydia's SUV. "I was hoping to get it done before you got here. I'm already inconveniencing you enough by asking you to pick me up."

"Like I said yesterday, I don't mind," she assured him. "I'm happy to give you a ride to work after our hike if you want, too."

"One of my coworkers is supposed to drop a work truck off here in about an hour, or as soon as his wife has time to give him a ride, so I should be good. Besides, I'll need the truck to get home later."

"Right, I guess you don't want to be stranded there until I get out of work." She looked down at her hands and grimaced. "Do you mind if I wash my hands before we go?"

"Come on in, I've got to wash mine too, and get Saffron's leash. Let's go in, girl, come on."

The last bit was directed toward Saffron, who had switched her attentions to the garbage bags. As soon as Jude spoke, she bounded toward the front door and sat in front of it, her tail wagging. Lydia smiled. There was something about seeing Jude and Saffron interact that always warmed her heart. It was obvious Jude loved his dog, and she adored him in return.

He opened the door and gestured her inside, but grabbed Saffron's collar before the dog could dart through with her muddy paws. While Lydia slipped off her boots, he wiped the dog's paws off on a towel he kept near the door for that purpose before finally letting her go inside. Saffron tolerated it in good humor and immediately shoved her nose into one of Lydia's empty boots.

The inside of Jude's house was clean and well cared for, but sparsely decorated – definitely a bachelor pad. There was a pair of dumb bells next to the couch, and more than a few issues of a fish and game magazine on the coffee table, Saffron's bed and the dog toys scattered across the floor added a homey touch to it.

She had only been here once before, shortly after his grandmother passed away, when she stopped by to drop off a care package from Iron and Flame for him to take to his parents when he stayed with them for a few days before the funeral. That was enough for her to remember where the bathroom was, though, and she hurried to wash and dry her hands before returning to the entranceway. Jude had washed his own hands at the kitchen sink and was currently trying to clip the leash to Saffron's collar. The dog was so excited that she couldn't hold still.

Amused, she watched until he finally managed to snag her collar and clip the leash to the ring. With the dog ready to go, they put their boots back on and headed outside. He didn't even pause to lock the door, something which she had come to the conclusion was just a man thing. Jeremy, her ex-husband, had never locked their door either. Sure, Quarry Creek was a small town and wasn't exactly rife with break-ins, but she couldn't imagine leaving her house without double checking that the deadbolt was in place.

"You can go ahead and put her in the back," she said as they reached the SUV. "I put the back seats down already, and I laid some old blankets out for her, so don't worry about the mud."

Saffron was thrilled when Jude told her to hop into the vehicle and started sniffing every nook and cranny she could find while Jude and Lydia buckled in. She started the engine, backed down the hill, and after checking for traffic, pulled out onto the road.

"Maybe if they can't figure out what's wrong with my truck, I'll sell it and get something like this," Jude said, turning around in the passenger seat to look at the SUVs interior. "All that space in the back is nice, and it's probably safer for Saffron than riding up front is."

"It's a good vehicle," she said. "Sometimes I feel a little guilty about having an SUV when I don't have kids and almost never use all the space, but whenever it snows, I remember why I needed something with four-wheel-drive. I don't know how you manage that driveway of yours after a snowstorm."

"I've spent a lot of time shoveling," he said. "Thanks again for picking me up, by the way. These last few weeks have been rough. Hopefully, today was the last of the bad stuff for a while."

"I meant to ask earlier, how was the will reading?"

He had been gone last weekend, the second weekend in a row, to attend his grandmother's will reading with his parents and his other relatives. She had never met his family, but knew his parents lived a couple hours away, and that he had been close to his grandmother when he was younger but hadn't seen her as much in recent years.

He grimaced. "It went about as well as expected. She left me a few knickknacks of my granddad's that I liked when I was a kid, and she made sure everyone else got a little something that was important to them, but all those years spent in that nursing home ate through everything she and my granddad made from their investments. My aunt and uncle were both pretty upset when they learned all the money was gone. I guess they were expecting to get a small fortune. If they'd spent any time visiting her, they would've known how expensive her care was and would have known what to expect."

"That sounds stressful," she said. "How is your dad holding up?"

"It's been tough for him, but he spent a lot of time with her right at the end, and she had been declining for a while—we all knew it was coming. He'll be all right. I'm glad my mom is there for him. I'll probably visit them again in the next couple of weeks, just to see if they need anything. Is anything new in your life? I feel like I've been too focused on my own life recently."

She wrinkled her nose. "Well, Jeremy wants to hire a company to make an advertisement for the restaurant. It's a professional company with a great portfolio, which is reflected in the price they quoted him. We set aside money for advertising, of course, but this ad would be a lot more than our advertising budget, and I'm not so sure the restaurant needs it. He thinks it's the best idea he's ever had, so we're at a bit of a stalemate."

"I can imagine those arguments aren't fun," he said. "I'm sure you'll figure out something you're both happy with, though, especially since it doesn't sound like either option would be actively *bad* for the restaurant."

They kept chatting as they drove to the trailhead and started their hike. Something about talking to Jude helped her feel better to a greater extent than talking to anyone else did, even her sister. She thought part of it was because Lillian was always trying to problem solve. She loved her sister, but she tended not to let anything go until they found a solution. With Jude, they could just bounce thoughts and ideas off of each other and move from one topic to the next without getting bogged down in what they were going to do. Being around him was just … easy.

They didn't finish their normal loop through the woods, giving in to the mud partway through, but it was still a nice way to spend the morning, and both of them were in high spirits by the time they got back to his house.

"Daniel still hasn't dropped the truck off," Jude said as she parked in his driveway.

Frowning, he took his phone out of his pocket and checked the screen. She watched as he tapped a notification for a new text message.

Alicia's not going to be able to give me a ride until later this afternoon. I'll see if Caleb can help out, otherwise I'll just swing by in the truck later this afternoon and you can just drop me off at my place before you head to work.

"Eh, we'll figure it out," he said as he typed out a quick reply. "It's still chilly out, even if it's not as bad as it was before. Do you want to come in for a cup of coffee before you head out, or do you have to get to work?"

"I have the evening shift today, so I'm not in any hurry," she said as she shut off her SUV. "Coffee sounds good."

While he let Saffron out of the back of the SUV, she grabbed her purse and started towards the front door. Within moments, the dog bounded past her, only to stop at the front stoop. Something about the dog's sudden stillness made Lydia jolt to a halt as well. It took her just seconds to see what had caught the dog's attention.

There was a red smear on the doorknob, and a smudge on the door just beneath it. Looking down, she saw a few dark red drops on the front stoop as well, just in front of Saffron's paws.

Blood.

TWO

"You can let yourself in," Jude called out as he approached. "It's not locked."

"Jude," she said. Saffron took a step forward, almost stepping on one of the drops of blood, and Lydia quickly grabbed her collar and pulled her back. "Look."

Out of the corner of her eye, she saw him jog the last few feet over to her. He came to a stop by her shoulder, and she could *feel* the moment he saw what she had noticed. He froze just like she had, then put a gentle hand on her elbow and pulled her back a step before moving in front of her.

"Wait out here with Saffron," he said, his tone taking on a seriousness that she had heard only once before.

"You're not going in there alone, are you?"

"You should get your phone out and call the police, just in case, but if someone needs help, they might not be able to wait for the authorities to arrive. I need to go in and see what happened."

"I'm coming with you."

She started feeling around in her purse one-handed for her phone, keeping the other hand on the dog's collar. Jude hesitated, then clipped the leash back onto Saffron's collar before pulling the dog away and tying her to the flagpole near the corner of the house. Lydia took the opportunity to grab her phone out of her purse, but hesitated, not sure if she should call 911 right now or not. Maybe they should see what they were dealing with first.

"Stay behind me, at least," he said as he returned from tying the leash to the flagpole. Saffron whined, the hackles on her back standing up.

She nodded once, briskly. As a game warden, he dealt with potentially dangerous people on a regular basis, and he would know how to react if someone was waiting for them in the house. She would stay out of the way, but she just didn't want him going inside by himself.

He reached for the door, then paused. Turning the knob would mean touching the bloody handprint on it. Backing away from the door, he caught her gaze and gestured around the side of the house. She followed him, brushing the top of Saffron's head with her fingers as they passed by the dog. She hoped Saffron would stay quiet. If someone was waiting for them in the house, they probably had heard the SUV pull up, but they might not know exactly where she and Jude were.

At the back door, Jude paused again, and they both examined the surrounding area for more blood, but everything seemed untouched. He pressed a finger to his lips, then pulled open the screen door. She held it for him while he turned the knob on the main door and pushed it open. It squeaked as it swung on its hinges, but other than that, the house was silent.

He stepped into the kitchen, and she followed behind him, making sure the screen door shut quietly before she turned to examine the kitchen.

Jude's kitchen was a small room with a once-white linoleum floor that was probably older than she was, pale blue countertops full of divots and scratches, and a microwave that she was pretty sure was the same model she'd had growing up. She was well aware that she could be a little snooty when it came to kitchens, but for once, the cooking potential of this room was the last thing on her mind. All she really cared about was that there was no blood staining the yellowish linoleum floor.

After a brief survey of the kitchen, Jude nodded toward the hallway, and she fell into step behind him. He seemed to know where every squeaky floorboard was, so she followed in his steps as closely as she could. The house was a ranch-style, with no upper story. The hallway out of the kitchen led directly to the living room and the front door. With Jude in front of her, she couldn't see what was around the corner, but from the way that he froze as soon as he reached the end of the hall, she knew it was bad.

After a painfully long moment, he moved out of her way, and she rounded the corner to see what he was looking at.

Someone was lying on the floor. A man she didn't recognize, with so much blood staining the carpet around his head that she knew in an instant he was dead.

"Who—" she started, but Jude pressed a finger to his lips, his eyes darting around the room. She understood immediately. Whoever did this might still be in here.

There was nowhere for someone to hide in the living room, but turning her back to the body made the back of her neck prickle as they started down the other hallway. This one led to the laundry room, bathroom, and bedroom. The laundry room and bathroom were both empty, and even the linen closet didn't hold anything but towels. They paused at the last door, the door to the bedroom, and their eyes met.

This was the last place someone could be hiding. Lydia swallowed, but despite the way her heart was thundering in her chest, she wasn't going to let Jude go in alone.

Still, as he reached for the doorknob, she took a step back. If someone *was* lying in wait, she would need time to react. But when Jude pulled the door open, nothing happened. No one leapt out at them, no gunshots rang out. He peeked through the door and made a small noise of surprise. She peered past him and, instead of another body, which she had been half expecting, she just saw a mess. Someone had dug through his closet, emptied the nightstand drawers, and had even torn the bedding off the bed and shoved the mattress off the box spring.

He entered the room, and she followed him over to the closet, where he kicked some clothing out of the way before frowning down at the closet's carpeted floor.

"What is it?" she whispered, still tense even though, by now, they knew the house was empty … if the body in the living room didn't count.

"I had a safe here. A small one, for documents. It's missing."

"So whoever did this knew where you kept your valuables?"

He gave a dry, helpless laugh. "That's the thing. There weren't any valuables in it. I kept a few tax documents in there, my Social Security card, a few drawings my niece made me when she was younger, the knickknacks my grandmother left me, but nothing worth money. Heck, Caleb knew that. A couple years ago, he was thinking about getting a safe for a pistol he inherited, and I let him look mine over to see if he liked the model."

"Caleb?"

He backed away from the closet and looked around the room again, like he was hoping to see something that would make everything make sense. "That's who the man in the living room is. Was. He's a good friend. We used to work together, but he quit to open a hunting and fishing supply store a few years ago."

He met her eyes. His own were wide, helpless, confused. When he turned without a word and went back to the living room, she followed him, and they stood over his friend's body together. One of the dumbbells she had seen earlier was lying on the floor not far from Caleb's body, and a glance was enough to tell her it had been used as the murder weapon. She felt sick to her stomach and had to back away from the scene to have any chance of forcing her nausea to subside.

"What happened?" Jude asked, his voice cracking. "I don't understand."

"Didn't your work friend who was supposed to drop off the truck say something about asking Caleb to help him in the text he sent you?" Lydia asked.

Jude blinked and slowly took his phone out of his pocket. She realized with a jolt that she had been clinging uselessly to her own phone all this time, and quickly opened the number pad to call 911. As the system patched her through to the dispatcher, she watched Jude read and reread the text message from his friend, and she wondered what in the world had happened here.

THREE

While they waited for the police to arrive, Lydia settled Saffron into her SUV, cracking the windows so the dog could look out but not *get* out, then led a stunned and confused Jude over to the SUV so he could lean against the hood. She had never seen him look so utterly lost before, and tried to imagine what she would be feeling if she got home to find a friend of hers murdered on her living room floor.

She couldn't wrap her head around it. It didn't feel real, even to her. Half an hour ago, they had been laughing as they hiked through the woods. Now, Jude's life had changed forever. She could barely comprehend it, and *she* wasn't the one who had lost a friend.

They heard the police vehicles before they saw them. She felt a prickle as the wailing sound of the sirens drew closer. It wasn't a cheerful noise, and it was one she had heard too often over the past few months.

Everything moved quickly after that. The police arrived and secured the house, making sure there was no lingering danger before they started documenting everything. Detective Bronner, who she recognized from a handful of interactions she'd had with him over the past few months, examined the crime scene before coming out to talk to her and Jude. They had been asked not to leave, and it was chilly enough that eventually they moved inside the SUV to wait. Now, after a brief greeting, Detective Bronner separated them, taking Jude across the yard to speak with him privately while she waited in the vehicle with Saffron.

"I'm still half convinced I'm going to wake up from this nightmare any moment," she murmured to the dog. "I guess it's a good thing we left when we did this morning, huh? I hate to think what would've happened if we had ended up cancelling the hike for some reason."

Of course, maybe this wouldn't have happened at all if they had been here. Maybe whoever broke in and killed Jude's friend had only done it because the driveway was empty, and they thought no one was home.

She frowned. That didn't make sense. Jude's friend would have driven here, which meant there should have been a vehicle in the driveway to scare away potential burglars. Maybe he had arrived only to find someone already in the house? But then, what had happened to his other friend, the one who had asked Caleb to help him drop off Jude's work truck? Her stomach clenched, and for the first time, it occurred to her that there might be another body somewhere. Between them and the police, they had checked every nook and cranny of the house, but the woods were right there, and a body could have been hidden anywhere in the trees.

She didn't have long to dwell on her newest concern, because Detective Bronner was coming back, and he was alone. She looked around the yard but didn't see where he had taken Jude. As the detective approached, she rolled down the window. He gave her a grim smile in greeting.

"I'd like to ask you a few questions, ma'am. Do you mind if I join you in there? Or if you'd be more comfortable, we can talk out here."

"No, you're welcome to sit in here with me where it's warm. Jude's dog is in the back, but she's friendly."

"Don't worry, I have a dog of my own. Great animals. Mine's a chocolate lab, and she's not the brightest, but she's darn loyal."

He went around to the other side of the SUV and opened the passenger door, pausing to let Saffron sniff his hand before he scratched her chest. The dog wagged her tail, panting happily as he got into the passenger seat and shut the door.

"It sounds like you've had an unpleasant morning, ma'am. Do you think you could walk me through it? Everything that happened from the time you arrived to when you called 911."

"Well, Jude's personal vehicle is in the shop, so we agreed that I'd pick him up a little after eight..."

She described her morning in as much detail as she could. He made a few notes and occasionally paused her to ask for clarification, but mostly, he just let her talk. When she was done, he glanced at his notepad and cleared his throat.

"Have you known Jude long?"

"I met him about five months ago, and we've been friends ever since. We meet up for hikes once or twice a week most weeks."

"Did anything about his behavior seem unusual to you when you got here this morning?"

"Not really. He seemed fine, despite the trash. He definitely didn't seem to think anything like *this* might happen."

Detective Bronner nodded slowly. The trash had been one of the things he had asked her a few extra questions about, but she hadn't been any help there. Whoever vandalized his yard was a mystery, and not a very important one compared to the murder.

"Are you familiar with any of his friends or coworkers?"

She shook her head. "No. I haven't met any of the people he works with, and I don't know anything about them other than whatever tidbits I've picked up from him talking about them."

"Are you aware of any enemies he might have? People who would want to target him for some reason? Any exes who might not be so happy about your presence in his life, people he's upset in the course of his job, coworkers he doesn't get along with?"

"I'm sure he's made some enemies during his time as a game warden, but he hasn't mentioned anyone specific. I don't really know anything about his dating history, either. We aren't romantically involved. I just want to clear that up, in case that's what you were thinking."

He nodded and made a note, then said, "Well, Ms. Thackery, thank you for your help. Rest assured that this case will be a priority for us. We may need you to go over some of this again or answer more questions at some point in the near future, so if you're planning on leaving town, I'd appreciate a heads-up."

"I don't have any trips planned any time in the near future," she assured him. "Are we free to go? Jude's not in trouble for anything, is he?"

He shook his head. "Your account matches up with his, and it's clear that neither of you were here when this happened. It's a good thing you entered the house before the two of you left, because it helps us narrow down the time frame the crime took place in."

Maybe the vandal leaving trash all over the place was a blessing in disguise, because now that she thought about it, it was lucky that she had seen with her own two eyes that there was no body on his living room floor when she went inside to wash her hands. She hated to think about the trouble he might have been in otherwise. Without her as a witness, he very likely would have been a suspect in his friend's murder.

After Detective Bronner gave her the all clear to go and left the SUV, she looked around for Jude again, and this time she spotted him chatting with an officer near one of the patrol cars. He worked with the police sometimes, so he must know some of the officers who had shown up today. She rolled down her window and waved, getting his attention, and after a brief word to the officer, he jogged over to her.

"The detective is all set?" he asked.

She nodded. "He said we can go. Do you need a ride anywhere? What are you planning on doing after this?"

He frowned, as if he hadn't considered it yet. "I don't know. I guess I'd better grab a room at the motel and let my supervisor know I need another personal day. I don't know what to do next. Maybe see if I can track down Daniel and ask him what happened, and if he ever got in touch with Caleb about the truck, though the police might manage it before I can."

Right ... his house was a crime scene. He couldn't stay here tonight, and probably not for the next few nights either. The thought of him sitting alone in a motel room after all of this was depressing.

"Why don't you come stay with me for a couple of days?" she offered. "Saffron is welcome too, of course. The couch pulls out into the most uncomfortable bed you've ever slept on, but I have a fenced in yard for Saffron, and not to toot my own horn, but I've been told I'm a pretty good cook."

He gave a weak chuckle, but he hesitated. "Are you sure? I don't know how long it'll be. I don't want to inconvenience you."

"I mean it," she said. "I'm not joking about how uncomfortable that pull-out couch is, but I'm sure you'll be more comfortable leaving Saffron there while you're at work, and I can guarantee you it's a lot cleaner than any motel you're going to find around here. Besides, you shouldn't be alone after all of this."

"Well, then, I accept," Jude said. "Let me go talk to one of the officers I know and see if they can grab some of Saffron's things for me before we go."

She watched him walk away, idly petting Saffron as the dog poked her head up into the front. She couldn't remember the last time she'd had a house guest who wasn't her sister, let alone an overnight guest. It was going to take some getting used to, but she didn't regret offering her couch to Jude. What happened here was going to stay with both of them for a long time, and she didn't think it would be good for either of them to try to process it alone.

FOUR

By the time Jude and Saffron were settled into her house, Lydia had to go to work. It felt strange leaving the two of them behind when she left. It wasn't that she didn't trust Jude with her things while she was gone, but it was just odd to know someone was in her house while she was at work.

She tried to focus on her duties and nothing else while she was at Iron and Flame. What happened at Jude's house had yet to hit the town's radar, and she wasn't going to be the one to bring it up. She had a lot on her mind but did her best to shove it aside and focus only on the familiar art of searing steaks and filleting trout and picking the best scallops out of the bunch.

After the kitchen closed that evening, she stayed behind the grill to whip up dinner for her and Jude before heading home. It had been a busy day at the restaurant, but the upside was that Jeremy hadn't had time to harangue her about the advertisement again. She had arrived late enough, and he had been exhausted enough that he just left without a word when she got there. They would have to figure it out eventually, but it was the last thing she wanted to think about today.

The lights were on in her house when she pulled into the driveway, and the warm glow was welcoming. After the gruesome scene from earlier, she didn't think she would have been comfortable walking into a dark house so late at night. Knowing Jude and Saffron were there gave her peace of mind.

She let herself in the front door and was greeted by Saffron. The dog was overjoyed to see her, as if it had been weeks since their hike, not hours.

"Why, yes, I missed you too," Lydia cooed as she slipped off her sneakers and kicked them into the closet. Her hands were full with her purse and the to-go bag from Iron and Flame; she could organize her shoe stand better later.

Jude came around the corner from the living room and greeted her. "She could tell when you were getting close," he said. "We had the TV on, but she perked right up about thirty seconds before you pulled in."

"She must know the sound of my engine," Lydia said, touched. "I brought food home, but if you already ate, it will keep until lunch tomorrow."

"I was going to offer to order a pizza. You didn't have to do that."

She set her purse down on the end table in the entrance way and walked into the kitchen, both Jude and Saffron following her. "It only took me a few minutes to whip up. I bring food home from the restaurant frequently, and making a second order was barely any extra work. It's just steak, potatoes, and a green salad. Nothing fancy."

He raised an eyebrow as he opened one of the boxes, and looked from the food inside to her. The amused, skeptical look made her give a huff of laughter.

"All right, maybe it's a little fancy. I've been spoiled by my own restaurant, haven't I?"

He chuckled. "You're a skilled chef. Most of us can't whip up a steak that looks this good in a few minutes like it's nothing."

"Let me get some real plates and silverware out, those to-go boxes are terrible. How was your afternoon? Is Saffron settling in well?"

"I think so. She has been enjoying all of the new smells. She got up on your couch a few times, but I've been trying to keep her off."

"Maybe we can lay down some blankets. As long as her paws aren't muddy, I don't mind too much."

"She really likes looking out the living room window and watching people walk by. We don't get that many pedestrians where we live, so it's been giving her plenty of entertainment. As far as she's concerned, this is an exciting surprise vacation."

"How are *you* holding up? Have the police called with any new information?"

He shook his head. "Nothing from them. I did get in touch with Daniel, though."

"Oh, that's a relief," she said as she sat down at the kitchen table. Jude joined her, and they each took a moment to move the food from the to-go containers to their plates while Saffron watched hopefully from a few feet away. "He's all right?"

Jude nodded. "He said he never ended up getting in touch with Caleb. He thinks Caleb might have already passed away when he tried to call him."

"Wait, if he didn't ask Caleb to help him drop off your work truck, then why was Caleb there?"

"I don't know. I've been wondering the same thing," Jude said. He cut a bite out of his steak but didn't eat it right away. "Daniel said the police already spoke to him, so hopefully they will be able to figure it out. I've known Caleb for a long time, but we never had the sort of friendship where we would let ourselves into each other's house, especially without calling first. I can't imagine what he was doing there, or how it ended so badly."

"Did you tell the police about your missing safe?" she asked.

"I did, and I told them what the contents were, but getting it back isn't a priority for me. I should be able to replace most of it. It might be a pain, but I'm a lot more concerned with finding out what happened than with getting some papers back."

"I know you already talked about all of this with the police, and I understand if you don't want to go through it again with me, but do you have any idea *who* might have done this? Detective Bronner asked me if you had any irate exes or coworkers you didn't get along with, and it made me realize I don't actually know all that much about your past. There have to be some people who have gotten upset with you for doing your job. I'd imagine game wardens aren't well liked by everyone they come across."

"Oh, I've ticked plenty of people off while doing my job," he said. "No one likes getting fined or arrested. My department will be sharing my case files with the police. Derek Chambers's case is the most recent one that stands out—he's the one who shot a deer in his neighbor's yard in the middle of town and for some reason thought he would get away with it. We settled that last month, though. I get along with all of my coworkers, and as far as exes go…" He hesitated. "I'm not going to lie, my last relationship didn't end well, but I haven't spoken to her in well over a year. It's hard to imagine she would be involved in this."

Lydia's curiosity was piqued. "You can tell me if it's none of my business, but what happened? Does she live in Quarry Creek?"

"She lives in Afton Fork." Afton Fork was the next town over, a small but ritzy community with some nice stores Lydia sometimes visited when the shopping bug bit her. "I don't mind talking about it. It's something I think you will understand, actually, probably better than some of my other friends did. Her name was Madison Donner. We were pretty serious, together for a little over three years and starting to talk about big things like marriage until I found out that early on in our relationship, but after we had agreed to be exclusive, she was still going on dates and spending the night with other men. I ended things, of course. I'm not going to commit to someone I can't trust, and I don't think there's any way to regain trust after something like that."

Lydia grimaced in sympathy. "I'm so sorry."

"That's not the worst of it. She ... went completely insane. That's the only way I can think to describe it. She let herself into my house multiple times to try to convince me to take her back, and I had to change all of the locks. It got to the point where I was worried she was going to hurt Saffron, so I went forty minutes out of my way each day to drop her off at a doggy daycare before work. Madison would come to the office a few times a week and make a scene, and she seemed to show up wherever I went. She would park outside my house and just watch the place, and every time I blocked her number, she would get a new one just so she could call me. It got bad enough that I got a restraining order against her, which seemed to do the job because I haven't heard from her since. That's one of the reasons I knew how serious it was when I found out one of your employees was stalking you. I've been there, and I know what it's like. No one should go through that."

"I can't even imagine what that must have been like," she said. "She was someone you trusted, and she betrayed that completely."

"It was not the best time in my life, but I've managed to get back to a good level of normal by now. Last I heard, she was in a relationship with someone else, which might explain why she stopped harassing me. It's been long enough that I would be surprised if she started up again."

Not for the first time, she was glad her divorce with Jeremy had been so simple and free of drama. He might drive her crazy sometimes, but at least she had never been afraid for her life around him.

She just hoped Jude was right to dismiss Madison so easily. *Someone* had broken into his house and killed his friend. At the moment, their only two suspects were an irate poacher and a crazy ex, and out of those two options, she knew which one she would put her money on.

FIVE

The next morning, she woke up to the sound of something sniffing at the gap under her bedroom door. She lay in bed for a breathless moment, wondering if a bear had somehow gotten into her house, then remembered that Saffron and Jude were here. She got out of bed, put on her bathrobe and slippers, and opened the bedroom door to Saffron's enthusiastic greeting.

"Saffron, don't bother Lydia," Jude hissed, poking his head around the corner of the kitchen to look down the hall. When he saw Lydia petting the dog, he gave a sheepish grin. "Sorry, I didn't want her to wake you up."

"I usually get up around now anyway," she said, giving the dog one last pat before straightening up. "How was your night?"

"You were telling the truth about that couch," he said. "I almost think I might be better off ignoring the pullout tonight and just sleeping on it as a couch. If you don't mind me staying the night again, of course."

"Not at all, you're welcome to stay, and yeah, you your back might thank you for that."

"The bed might be zero stars, but the company is a lot better than it would be at the motel," he said with a grin. "Oh, before I forget, I got a call from the auto shop. My truck is ready to pick up. I hate to ask, because I feel like I've inconvenienced you a lot lately as it is, but would you mind giving me a ride there on your way to the restaurant so I can pick it up?"

"Sure, we'll just have to leave a little early. We should be out of the house in about forty-five minutes."

They made it out of the house right on time. While Lydia went through her morning routine, Jude took

Saffron on a walk around the block to get some of her energy out. She was a little nervous about leaving the dog alone in the house all day, but he had managed to convince one of the police officers to pack up a few of the dog's toys, and there wasn't much in Lydia's house that she could destroy unless she decided to eat the walls or something equally as unlikely. They left a nature program playing on a low volume on the TV for her, and Jude assured her that Saffron would probably spend the day sleeping.

The auto shop wasn't far from Iron and Flame, a couple of blocks further east along the main road. Jude's truck was sitting in front of the office when they pulled in, and she gave it a critical look as she shut off her engine.

"Did they say what was wrong with it?"

"There was water in the gas tank," he said. "They aren't sure why; they said they couldn't find any leaks in the tank or in any of the lines. They drained the tank and flushed the system and told me to bring it back in if it happens again."

"Sounds about right," Lydia said. "I had a lot of issues with them tracking down the problems in my old car. I hope you don't end up getting stranded somewhere. Are you good for me to just drop you off here?"

"Let me run in and get the keys to make sure it actually starts."

She waited in her SUV while he went inside the auto shop. It was strange spending so much time with him—strange, but nice. Doing these mundane activities together felt natural, and she was beginning to realize how much she had missed having someone to just live her life with.

The sound of a car horn going off made her glance in the rearview mirror, which reflected the street behind her. A silver SUV of a similar model to her own was parked along the curb, and it looked like it had tried to pull out into traffic. She watched as it backed up and let the vehicle that cut it off pull forward. There was a line of traffic stopped at a red light, and she imagined she could sense the driver's frustration even from here. Traffic in Quarry Creek wasn't always this bad, but it had definitely been getting worse over the past few years. It was a sign of their growing tourism industry, which was good for the many small businesses in town, but it could be irritating as a local who just wanted to get around.

Jude came out of the auto shop with his keys in hand and got into his truck. She waited until she saw it start, then rolled down her window. He did the same from his side.

"All good?" she asked.

He gave her a thumbs-up. "Runs like new. Thanks again for dropping me off. If I have time during lunch, I'll swing by your place and check on Saffron, if that's all right."

"That's fine," she said. "Actually, hold on, let me give you a key." She took it off her keychain and got out of her vehicle to carry it around to Jude. "There you go. I have a spare, so don't worry about locking me out."

"Thanks," he said. "I'll let you know if I do end up stopping by. I'd better get going now, I'm going to have a lot of work to catch up on, and I know everyone I work with is going to want to talk about what happened before they let me get to it."

They exchanged goodbyes, and he backed out of the spot, pulling out of the parking lot just as the light at the intersection turned green. She hurried to get back into her SUV so she could catch the light as well. Giving him the key had been a leap of faith, but she didn't want Saffron to have to be alone in a strange place all day if she didn't have to. She hoped she wouldn't come to regret it, but she didn't think she would. She thought she could trust Jude.

She drove the few blocks down the street to Iron and Flame. This early, before the restaurant opened, the parking lot was empty. She parked toward the middle of the lot, wanting to leave the best spaces for their guests, but paused before she reached the door when she heard another vehicle pull into the lot. She turned around, expecting to see one of her employees arriving a little bit early but instead saw the same silver SUV that she had seen across the street from the auto shop a few minutes ago. It was a weird coincidence, and she wondered if it was someone she knew, but the vehicle just pulled far enough into the parking lot to do a U-turn before it pulled back out on the road.

Shaking off the coincidence, she unlocked the restaurant's doors and let herself in. Almost as if it was timed, her phone started ringing the moment she crossed over the threshold. She pulled her phone out of her purse and glanced at the name on the caller ID.

Jeremy. And she knew exactly what he was calling about. With a sigh, she answered the call, put it on speakerphone, and carried her phone with her as she went into the kitchen and started turning on the lights.

"Before you ask, I still haven't decided," she said, getting right to it.

He jumped in without missing a beat. "The quote's only good until the end of the month, Lydia. I know it's a lot of money, but think how many people an ad like that could reach. We have one of the nicest restaurants in this part of the state. We could be huge, if only we can get our name out there."

"It's more than triple our yearly advertising budget, and that money has to come from somewhere..."

Her shift started with an argument and ended with one. Unable to convince her over the phone, Jeremy came in half an hour before her shift ended and continued the conversation, apparently unable to understand why she was reluctant to spend so much money on an advertisement that might not end up paying off. They got nowhere with their second argument of the day, and she left work in a sour mood. A mood that only got worse when she saw the numerous long scratches in the dark paint of her SUV.

Someone had keyed her car.

SIX

She went back inside the restaurant to ask her employees if any of them had seen what happened, then got into yet another argument with Jeremy when he overheard the wrong part of her question and thought she was accusing him of keying her car. They usually got along better than this, but the disagreement about the advertisement was leaking into other parts of their lives now.

No one had seen anything, and she hadn't parked close enough to the door for the security cameras to pick it up, but she wasn't prepared to just let it go, so she made a report to the police. She spent what felt like a wasted half an hour waiting for an officer to show up and take her statement, only to be told there wasn't much they could do unless someone witnessed what happened, and then spent the drive home on the phone with her insurance company, trying to see if they would cover the repairs.

By the time she got home, she had all but forgotten Jude and Saffron were staying with her, and she spent an embarrassingly long time staring at the truck in her driveway, wondering if she had pulled up to the wrong house.

It was just one of those days. She sat in her vehicle in the driveway for a few minutes, taking the deep, slow breaths that were all she remembered from her yoga phase during culinary school. The scratches on her vehicle were annoying, but they weren't the end of the world. The disagreement with Jeremy about the advertisement was also annoying, but it would probably have been resolved by now if she hadn't been so distracted these past few days and actually put her mind to coming up with a compromise. She needed to get a grip on things. There was no reason to spend the rest of the day being miserable.

With everything that had happened, she completely forgot she had given the key to Jude, but thankfully, he noticed her standing on the front stoop. While she was looking at the keys on her keychain, wondering if she had lost her mind, he opened the door for her. Saffron tried to push past him, and he bent down to grab her collar, pulling her back to give Lydia space to walk inside.

"I think she's even more excited to see you than she was to see me."

Lydia smiled, the dog's cheer infectious despite her less than stellar mood.

"Well, I'm glad to see her too," she said as she stepped into the house and shut the door behind her. Saffron was wagging her tail so hard that her whole body was wagging with it. Jude released her collar, and Lydia spent a few moments greeting the dog before she took off her shoes and gave Jude a sheepish smile.

"Sorry, I feel like I always say hi to Saffron before I say hi to you."

"I'm used to her stealing the show," he said. "How was your day?"

"It was terrible," she admitted. "Yours?"

"Not great either, but we can get to that in a minute," he said. "You want to talk about what's going on with you?"

She grimaced. "Just more arguments with Jeremy about the advertisement he wants to make, and then when I left work today, I discovered someone scratched up my SUV."

He winced in sympathy. "How bad is it?"

"We can go out and look at it together if you want. It's pretty bad."

Leaving Saffron inside, they left through the front door and walked over to her SUV together. Jude let out a low whistle at the sight of the scratches. They ran from the front to the back of her SUV on both sides.

"That can't have been an accident. Did anyone see anything?"

"Nope. I filed a police report, but it doesn't sound like they'll be able to do much. My insurance should cover it once they receive the report, though. That's the only silver lining."

"I don't know what's going on with Quarry Creek recently," he said. "I was about to head out to the state park to do a routine patrol when I got a call from Detective Bronner. Someone dumped paint all over my driveway at some point during the night, and they discovered it this morning. I had to go down to the station and deal with that. They're taking it seriously because of the murder."

She pursed her lips, staring at her SUV. "Do they think it's connected?"

"I think it's more that they want to cover their bases in the off chance that it's connected," he said.

"What if all of these coincidences aren't coincidences after all?"

"What do you mean?" he asked, raising his eyebrows.

They headed back toward the house, and she talked as she walked. "I know this might sound a little crazy, but think about it. The water in your truck's gas tank, the trash someone threw all over your lawn, and the paint someone dumped on your driveway. Not counting the murder, that's three separate incidents you've experienced in the past week. And today, I swear a silver SUV followed me from the auto shop to the restaurant. I didn't think much of it at the time, but then this happened to my vehicle. And of course, the murder. I don't know if that's connected, but what if all of this vandalism is?"

"I'm not saying you're wrong." He paused to open the door for her, and both hurried in before Saffron could get out. "But why would someone target both of us?"

"I have no idea. It seems personal, though, doesn't it? Are you sure your ex isn't still hung up on you? Maybe she thinks we're dating and she's upset about it."

"Like I said, I haven't spoken to her for over a year, so I have no idea what's going on in her life, but as far as I know, she's moved on. If you want to look her up online, we can. Since we're talking about exes, you don't think Jeremy would do something like this, do you?"

She shook her head. "No, it's not his style, and I don't see why he would target you, anyway. It's not like we're dating, and even if we were, he wouldn't care. All he cares about at the moment is that stupid advertisement, and scratching up my car isn't going to help him get what he wants."

"Well, we can look Madison up, but the last I heard, she was in a long-term relationship and seemed stable."

It was the only lead they had to go on, so they got her laptop out and logged into her social media account, since Jude had Madison blocked on his. He typed in her name into the search bar, *Madison Donner*, and clicked on the correct profile.

"Oh, shoot," he said.

Lydia stared at the most recent public post on the woman's page. It was a photo of a platinum blonde woman with a pixie-like face and long, neon pink fingernails standing in front of a silver SUV with a body of text reading, *Please help! As many of you know, Hugh and I went our separate ways, and he left me with nothing. I'm living out of my car. Any and all charity is appreciated. You can donate at...* and then an email address.

"That's the grocery store parking lot," Jude said. "Not the one in Afton Fork. The one here."

"I recognize it," she agreed. "Her SUV … it's the same one that followed me to the restaurant this morning. And she posted this on Tuesday, which is the day your truck stopped working, so we know she was in town then, at the very least. I know it isn't proof she did something to your truck, but…"

"You might be right. I wish you weren't. I had hoped I was done dealing with her. I need to give my friend Daniel a call. His wife is still close with her, so maybe she'll know more about what's going on."

She squeezed his shoulder. "Hopefully, we're wrong. But if she's fixating on you again, it's better to know about it. Maybe it's a good thing you're staying here. She doesn't know where I live, which means she doesn't know where you are either."

"Let's just hope it stays that way."

SEVEN

Over dinner, which was a rare treat of pizza since she had been in too much of a hurry to get away from Jeremy to take the time to bring something home, and neither of them particularly felt like cooking or going out to pick something up, they went over everything that had happened over the past few days from their new perspective. If they were right and the vandalism was all committed by one person, then it went from annoying to terrifying.

Because if the vandalism was all related, then maybe the murder was too, and if whoever had a grudge against Jude was willing to kill, then there was a real chance one of them might be next.

Hoping to get more information about his ex's situation, Jude called Daniel to see if he and his wife were available to meet with them. Daniel replied within minutes, but said they were out of town for the evening and offered to meet before work the next morning instead. Jude took him up on the offer, though to Lydia, the wait felt like an eternity. She wanted to know *now* exactly what they were facing.

If their hypothesis was right and Madison had started stalking Jude again, then preventing her from knowing where Jude was staying was paramount. After a serious discussion, they decided it wasn't worth the risk to take Saffron on a walk around the block, even though the dog was bored from being cooped up all day. Instead, they made do with playing fetch in the backyard. The yard was really too small for the purpose, but it was better than nothing. Saffron was a unique-looking dog, and the risk that Madison would spot her was too high, even if she and Jude bundled up to disguise their faces.

In order to meet with Daniel and Alicia, his wife, before everyone had to get to work the next morning, they woke up at seven thirty. All of the fun banter from the morning before was gone. Instead, they got ready to go in silence. Lydia double-checked that her house was locked up tight before they got into her SUV.

Daniel and his wife lived in a house a couple of blocks from Quarry Creek's small downtown area. Daniel was already in his work uniform when he answered the door. He welcomed them in, and Jude introduced him to Lydia.

"Daniel and I have worked together for years. I think we both started there in the same month, in fact."

"It's nice to meet you," Lydia said, shaking his hand.

"It's nice to meet you too. I've heard a lot about you." He looked up the stairs and raised his voice, "Alicia, they're here."

Alicia, when she came down, gave Lydia a flustered but friendly smile. "Sorry about that. I work at the library. We open at nine, so I've got to leave in about half an hour. I was trying to get ready before you got here. Come on in and sit down."

"Thanks for letting us come over so early," Jude said. He and Lydia sat on the loveseat together, while Daniel and Alicia took the couch opposite them.

"It sounded important, and after what happened to Caleb... Well, we've got to stick together, don't we?"

"This isn't what I wanted to ask you about, but you haven't heard anything more about that, have you?" Jude asked. "I know it's only been a couple of days, but it's bothering me. I can't understand why Caleb was in my house. Are you sure he didn't say anything to you?"

Daniel shook his head. "I've been wondering the same thing, but he never got back to me when I texted him, and after hearing the timeline from you, I'm pretty sure he had already been killed when I texted him to see if he could help me drop the work truck off at your place."

"Caleb used to work for the DNR too, didn't he?" Lydia asked. She was trying to keep all of this straight, but it was hard to do since she didn't know any of these people.

Daniel nodded. "That's right. He quit a couple years ago to open a store, but he still met us for drinks most weeks, and we were all still buddies. Well, he hadn't been around as much lately. I think his store has been having financial troubles, and he was too embarrassed to ask one of us to pay for him when we went out. I wish he had; we would've been happy to do it. He started working for the DNR at about the same time Jude and I did, so we went way back. We were all there when Jude went through that whole mess with Madison, which is what you're here to talk about, right?"

Jude nodded. "I know Alicia stayed in contact with her. Lydia and I have both been dealing with some vandalism, and last night we realized it might be connected. I looked Madison up on a hunch, and I saw from a recent post of hers that she's had some life changes recently. Do you know what's going on with her? The last thing I want is to have to deal with her again on top of everything else."

"I'm not as close to her as I used to be, but I'm still friends with her online," Alicia said. "I know she went through a bad breakup a couple weeks ago. I don't know the details, but what I think happened is she quit her job and was living in her boyfriend's house for free in exchange for taking care of his kids. He kicked her out, and now she has no savings and nowhere to go."

"Has she tried to contact you?"

"She sent me a text message last week, but since she was asking for money and asking about you, I ignored it."

"She asked about me?" Jude asked. His voice was tense, and Lydia reached out to touch his knee. From her brief experience with one of her employees stalking her, she was aware of how bad the situation could be.

"Maybe I should have said something, but I didn't think much of it at the time. It's been so long since all that happened." Alicia frowned and picked up her phone, scrolling down the screen. "Let me see if I can find the message... Here it is. She asked me if I knew if you were seeing anyone, and if you still lived in the same house. Like I said, I never responded. But she might have reached out to other people as well."

Jude looked like he had just gotten the worst news imaginable. Lydia knew he had been hoping Madison had nothing to do with this, but if she had been asking people about him, then it was probably a futile hope.

"Hold on, do you think she had something to do with what happened to Caleb?" Daniel asked. "That still doesn't make any sense. Why would she and Caleb be at your house? Why would she kill him?"

Alicia spoke up hesitantly. "I didn't say anything, because I knew it would just upset Jude, but when we hosted that game night here last fall, Caleb confessed that he and Madison had been seeing each other on the side. He asked me if I would be open to inviting her to our next gathering. I told him absolutely not, but I wouldn't be surprised if that was what led to the relationship between her and her boyfriend failing. I don't know why she would murder Caleb, or why they would be at your house, but the two of them being together doesn't surprise me."

EIGHT

There wasn't much to say after that. Daniel and Alicia had to finish getting ready for work, and she and Jude had to get back to Lydia's house so Jude could get his truck and leave on time for his own shift. As they got back into her SUV, she refrained from saying anything about the quality of his friends, though she thought he could do better. She couldn't imagine why they kept in touch with a woman who had *stalked* him, for goodness sakes.

"I'll swing by the police station when I get out of work and talk to them about what we learned this morning," Jude said as she started the SUV. "It seems like I've been out of the loop recently."

She considered how their theory might fit with the knowledge that Madison was without a doubt worming her way back into Jude's circle of friends. "Do you think Madison might have wanted something from your house? Would she have had a reason to take your safe?"

He shook his head, then shrugged. "I don't think so. I don't see what she could do with the deed to my house or the title to my car, since they're reported as stolen and will be useless to her. What else could she want? My tax documents? A drawing of my niece's favorite cartoon character? I don't know, maybe we're on the wrong track with her. If Caleb was seeing her, not only after everything I went through with her but while he *knew* she was dating someone else, then he isn't the same person I thought I was friends with for all those years. Maybe he was involved in something criminal and got in over his head. I wouldn't have thought he would get himself in that sort of trouble, but I wouldn't have thought he would start seeing her either."

"Maybe we're missing something. We can try to brainstorm some more this evening, if you want."

"Yeah, I suppose I should try to focus on my job for now." He checked his watch. "I should be just in time. I meant to ask you earlier, do you want me to take your SUV in with me today? One of my coworkers has a cousin who owns a body shop not far from the office. I can drop it off there and get a ride to work while he gets you a quote. You could drive the truck to the restaurant today."

"Are you sure? I don't like driving around like this, but it can wait until I have time to take it in myself."

"I'm happy to do it. If Madison's the one who scratched it up, then I feel like it's partially my fault."

It would save her some time, so she agreed, and when they got back to her house, they traded keys. She made sure to take the key to the restaurant off of her keychain, then said goodbye to Jude.

The good thing about working the morning shift was that she didn't have to worry about Jeremy ambushing her the second she stepped through the doors, though she knew there was a good chance he would come in early to continue their argument from yesterday. Still, it was a relaxing shift, though she knew it would start picking up tonight. Friday nights were their second busiest shift of the week.

They were preparing to make some changes to their seasonal menu, so she and Chartreuse, a sous chef who had been working there almost from the beginning, spent the morning discussing their options for the new dishes and making a list for Jeremy to look through and approve. She hoped he wouldn't be petty and veto her choices just because they disagreed on the advertisement he wanted to make.

She decided to get a second opinion on the ad and asked Chartreuse what she thought about it. She didn't go into details about the finances beyond mentioning it was out of their budget, and she tried to fairly lay out the pros and cons for both sides, without making it obvious which side she was on. The last thing she wanted was for any of their employees to feel like they had to pick sides between her and Jeremy, and she knew her ex-husband felt the same way. It was one of their iron-clad rules, something they had agreed upon even before their divorce, when they first opened the restaurant.

Chartreuse pursed her lips as she prepared a skillet of rosemary and garlic roasted potatoes. "If it brought in more business during the week, that would be nice. It gets pretty slow here, especially earlier in the week. If it made the weekends busier, we might need to start thinking about hiring some more staff. You and Jeremy and Hank have been making it work with the three of you on rotation so far, but there are times when it would be nice to have another chef in the kitchen, or some more people to help prepare ingredients or run orders out."

"Have you and the others been feeling stressed?" Lydia asked.

"Weekends have been getting busier and busier pretty steadily all year. I'm not complaining, I just don't know how much more we can take before we need some more hands on deck. I understand it doesn't necessarily make sense to hire new employees when half the shifts during the week are so slow you could hear a pin drop in the dining area. It would be hard to find people who would be willing to only work weekends."

"I'll bring it up with Jeremy," Lydia promised, already starting to problem solve for a problem she hadn't even known they had. Now that Chartreuse brought it up, things *were* a little unbalanced. Weekend shifts were hellish—she was lucky Jeremy had been willing to take them more often lately, though she knew that would change when he started dating someone again. And the morning shifts in the earlier part of the week were extremely slow, sometimes to the point where she spent more time standing around in the kitchen and chatting with her employees than actually cooking.

Maybe they could run an advertising campaign specifically encouraging people to come in for lunch on the weekdays, instead of running a generalized ad about the restaurant. It was true that they didn't really need the added business on weekends, but earlier in the day on weekdays was a market that could grow, and if it paid off, they could use the extra revenue to hire some new employees. Instead of an expensive television ad, they could do a focused marketing campaign online—it might be a little cheaper, and they could help the restaurant in a more targeted way.

She wanted to think it over a little more, but she thought her idea might be a good compromise. Hopefully, Jeremy would feel the same.

That was one problem solved. If only figuring out who had killed Caleb was so easy.

Jeremy was uncharacteristically late to his shift that evening, so he didn't have time to hound her about the advertisement, which was a relief since she wanted to figure out the details before bringing it up. Still, she made peace by telling him she had been thinking about the ad and would talk to him this weekend so they could figure it out. He apologized for going off on her yesterday, and by the time she left just after five, it was a lot later than she expected to be leaving the restaurant, but she was feeling better about things than she had in a long time.

When she spotted Valerie sitting at the bar, her mood improved even more. Valerie came in most days after she got out of work to grab a drink or get take-out, and she and Lydia chatted whenever their schedules coincided. Lydia had introduced her to some of her mutual friends, and she and Sierra had hit it off, so sometimes they came in together. It was nice having one or both of them come in to shoot the breeze with her sometimes, and she wasn't in a huge hurry today, despite how late Jeremy had been, so she headed over to the bar to talk with Valerie.

Her steps faltered when she got a good look at the woman her friend was animatedly talking with. Platinum blonde hair, long pink fingernails, and a pixie-like face. She had only ever seen a photograph of the woman online, but she was almost certain the woman Valerie was talking to was Madison, Jude's ex and the woman who might have murdered Caleb.

NINE

"There she is! Lydia, come over here and say hi."

Valerie spotted her and waved her over. Lydia approached hesitantly, trying to figure out if this woman really was Madison or if she was mistaken.

"I'm glad you're still here, because I was hoping I would get a chance to introduce you. We were talking, and she said she absolutely loves your cooking." She turned to the blonde woman. "This is Lydia, and she's a *great* chef. She really loves what she does, and she's always happy to talk to her guests."

That was true ... usually. Not when said guest might have murdered someone and almost certainly keyed her SUV. Still, she pasted on a smile and said, "I'm on my way out, but I've got a few minutes to talk if you have any questions about the kitchen or the restaurant. Like Valerie said, I'm Lydia. What's your name?"

The woman's lips curved up in a smile that didn't reach her eyes and extended a slender hand. "I'm Madison. You know, I think we have a mutual friend. You wouldn't happen to know a Jude Holloway, would you?"

Lydia shook her hand mechanically. She had no idea where to go from here. Her hunch that this was Madison was correct, but what did the woman want? Was she a jealous ex, or a murderous psychopath? She didn't want to make a scene, but she was also aware that she could be in very real danger from this woman if she was the one responsible for Caleb's gruesome death.

She decided playing dumb might be the safest way to go, at least for now. "Jude? Yeah, I've known him for a few months. Did he recommend the restaurant to you?"

"You could say that. I'm just happy to finally meet the woman he's been spending so much time with. I should be heading out now, but thanks for the chat. Tell Jude I said hi."

Madison hopped off her stool and walked away from the bar, flipping her hair over her shoulder as she went. Lydia stared after her, discomfited.

"I didn't know she knew Jude," Valerie said. "That was weird. Sorry, I thought she just wanted to meet the chef."

"You couldn't have known," Lydia said. "Have you seen her in here before?"

"No, I haven't. She was sitting at the bar when I got here, and I said hi because it's the polite thing to do. We started talking, which was when she asked if I knew you. Well, she didn't say your name, she asked about the lady chef who works here. But if she knows about you and Jude, she must have known who you were."

"She's his ex," Lydia explained. "I don't know how she knew who I was, though. I think she might have followed me to work yesterday, but for her to know I'm a chef, she must have done more digging."

She didn't like Madison's comment about meeting the woman Jude had been spending so much time with. Did she know Jude was staying with her temporarily, or had she been referring to their hikes? Either option was chilling.

"Yikes. I feel really bad now."

"Don't. It's not your fault. If you see her again, don't say anything to her, okay? Did you mention anything about where I live or my schedule?"

Valerie shook her head. "No, I don't think I gave away any personal information other than your name, and that you're the co-owner of Iron and Flame. Is there something going on with you and Jude?"

"It's complicated. If I have time later this weekend, we can get together. I'll tell you about it then, but I don't want to go into it here."

Even though Madison had left, she still felt on edge, and she wanted to get home, though she would only feel safe doing so after a long detour to make sure no one was following her.

After saying goodbye to Valerie, she made her way out to the parking lot and looked for her SUV. For a gut-sinking moment, she thought it had been stolen, but then she remembered she had driven

Jude's truck to work that morning. It was parked in her usual spot. She was a little worried Madison had done something to it, but there weren't any scratches on it, and it started with the turn of a key.

She kept her eyes peeled for a silver SUV as she pulled out of the parking lot, but either Madison was driving a different vehicle, or she had already left. She pulled out onto the road, going the opposite direction of her house, and drove around town until she was certain no one was following her.

Even so, she was wary about leaving Jude's truck parked in her driveway, and wished there was enough room to park in the garage. She really needed to get around to cleaning it out; it was full of moving boxes and furniture from the house she and Jeremy had owned together. She had been putting it off for years, but she couldn't put it off forever.

Jude wasn't there yet, so she let herself in and greeted Saffron, letting the dog out into the backyard to relieve herself while she texted him to make sure everything was all right. She wasn't too worried; his hours weren't as regular as hers, and he had mentioned he was going to talk to the police after work, which would delay him even if he had gotten done early.

She wanted to tell him about Madison in person, so she didn't bring it up in her text. To pass the time, she decided to start on dinner. She was due for a grocery shopping trip, so the pickings were slim, but a check of her freezer and cupboards told her she had all the ingredients she needed for a lasagna. It might not be the most gourmet lasagna she had ever made, but it would still be tasty and filling.

After starting the frozen ground beef defrosting in the microwave, she set a pot of salted water to boil on the stove for the noodles and opened a few cans of crushed tomatoes and tomato sauce so she could make a red sauce for the lasagna.

She started by sautéing garlic and onions in a pan with some butter, and once they were soft, she turned the heat down and added the last of her fresh herbs; rosemary and sage, marjoram and oregano. She heated them in the pan until they started to wilt, then added the canned tomatoes, a pinch of sugar, and some salt.

While the sauce simmered, she mixed ricotta cheese and cottage cheese together with an egg and some garlic powder, then set the mixture aside to grate the last of her cheese. After that, all she had to do was brown the meat, strain the noodles, and then put everything together.

She was sliding the assembled lasagna into the oven when Saffron, who had been lying just outside of the kitchen to watch her cook, jumped to her feet and trotted over to the front door. A moment later, she heard a key in the lock as Jude let himself in.

"It smells great in here," he said. "Are you cooking something?"

"I just whipped up a lasagna," she said. "I had the ingredients lying around, and I figured it's probably healthier than takeout."

"Oh man, I love lasagna. Dinner's on me next time, though. Can you come outside really quickly? I need your help with something."

Curious, she agreed, quickly wiping down the counters before she put her shoes on and followed him outside. He led her over to the SUV and then stopped, looking at her with a smile. It took her a second to realize that the scratches were gone.

"You got it fixed?" she said, her jaw dropping. "I thought you were just going to get a quote. What happened?"

He grinned, pleased by her surprise. "My coworker said his cousin could probably get it done in a couple of hours, so I ran it over to the body shop at lunch and had my coworker drop me off to pick it up after work."

"It looks so good," she said. "You can't even tell it was ever all scratched up. What do I owe you?"

He shook his head. "Nothing. I'm guessing Madison's the one who did it, which makes it my responsibility. You shouldn't have to pay the price for an ex of mine getting upset over nothing. Even if it wasn't her, I'm happy to do it as a thank you for letting me stay with you."

Some of her happiness dampened at the reminder of Madison.

"I hate to bring this up now, because this is a wonderful surprise, but you'll never guess who came into the restaurant today…"

TEN

Jude was livid at the news that Madison had confronted her, even though all the other woman had done was introduce herself. Given the circumstances, Lydia couldn't blame him. Even if Madison had nothing to do with Caleb's death, she was still someone who had stalked him to the point where he had to get a restraining order. Having her in their lives could spell nothing but trouble.

Still, they managed to have a nice evening together. She told him about her idea to drive more of the restaurant's business to the slower weekday lunch shifts, and he told her about his meeting with the police after work. They didn't have any new information to share about the murder, but they had told him that he should be able to go back home by Monday or Tuesday. She assured him that he was welcome to stay the weekend with her, and they decided to do their usual weekend hike tomorrow morning, since they both had the day off.

Saturday morning, she woke up to Jude making waffles—she had completely forgotten she had a waffle maker buried in the back of her pantry—and scrambling a single egg to add to Saffron's breakfast. She watched with her lips twitching as he chopped up the scrambled egg and mixed it in with her kibble. When he realized she was watching, his cheeks turned pink.

"She gets a special breakfast before we go on our long hikes," he explained.

"I think it's very sweet," she assured him.

They left for their usual trail late in the morning. The last few days had been overcast and humid, but not rainy, so the trail had dried out enough that it no longer resembled a mud pit.

It had the makings of a nice day, with some blue sky between the clouds. They set out with Saffron ranging ahead of them on her long leash. Despite everything; the murder, the vandalism, the details of the advertisement that she still had to work out with Jeremy, and the lingering unease at Madison's renewed presence in Jude's life, she felt … happy. She glanced over at Jude as they walked, wondering if she should take the leap and ask if he would go on a date with her. She was in her thirties, for goodness' sake. There was no reason she had to sit around and wait for a man to make the first move.

She would do it, she decided, but not right now. Not when he was going to be staying at her house through the weekend. It would make things awkward between them, no matter what he said.

They were only halfway up the big hill when Jude's cell phone started ringing. He ignored it at first, but when the person called back immediately, he paused to take his phone out of his pocket and check the caller ID. She could tell from the frown on his face that it was something important even before he spoke.

"It's the police."

He answered the call, and she took Saffron's leash from him so she could quietly call the dog back over to them, in case they had to head back to the parking lot. Saffron, who had no idea why they had stopped, looked up at her questioningly, her head cocked to the side as if asking if they were *really* done already.

"I understand," Jude said at last. "I'll be right there."

He ended the call, and Lydia asked, "What's going on?"

"The police made an arrest. They think they caught the person who has been vandalizing my house."

She clutched Saffron's leash more tightly. That was unexpectedly good news. "Who was it?"

"Derek Chambers."

"Why does that name sound familiar?"

"He's the one I told you about who shot the deer in his neighbor's yard in the middle of town a couple months ago. He got a conviction but no jail time, just a suspended hunting license and a fine. The police had an officer undercover across the street from my house, and they caught him red-handed when he pulled into my driveway with a bucket of blood in the car with him. I need to go down to the police station and deal with that, so it looks like we're going to have to cut our hike short again."

They started back down the trail, Saffron lingering behind them for a few moments until she decided that retracing their steps was just as fun as setting out in the first place had been.

"Do they think he's behind the murder as well?" Lydia asked.

"I don't know. I had to testify in court during his hearing, and I could tell he was pretty ticked off, but I didn't think he would come after me. He had to know it was a bad idea."

"Well, one would think he would know shooting a deer in the middle of town was a bad idea too," Lydia pointed out. "I've never even met the guy, but I'm pretty sure reason isn't his strong suit."

He chuckled. "You might have a point."

Having their hike cut short again was a bummer, but as they made their way back down the trail, Lydia felt nothing but relief. If Derek Chambers really was behind everything, then all of their worries were over.

They were almost back to the parking lot when Saffron's ears perked up and she tugged on the leash, wagging her tail. A moment later, Lydia caught sight of movement in the trees and realized someone else was on the trail coming their way. The trail was never super busy, but it wasn't uncommon for them to come across another hiker or two when they were out here. Still holding Saffron's leash, she called the dog over to her side to shorten the amount of leeway she had, then scratched the dog behind her ears, praising her.

She didn't even notice when Jude stopped, until he spoke in a low voice. "Are you kidding me?"

He sounded so upset that at first, she thought he was mad at her for some reason, but when she looked over at him, she saw that he was looking further down the trail, toward the person who was approaching them.

In an instant, she knew why he sounded so upset. The other hiker was none other than Madison. The other woman was striding up the path toward them, seemingly unsurprised to see them here.

"What are you doing here?" Jude asked as she approached.

She paused a few feet away from them, crossing her arms and giving Lydia a brief, dismissive look before focusing on Jude. "What? It's state land. It's open to the public."

"How did you know where we were? Have you been following me again?"

She laughed, a mean sound with absolutely no joy in it. "You're so self-centered, Jude. I thought it was a nice day for a walk, that's all."

"Stay away from me, and stay away from Lydia. Don't bother her at her restaurant again. She told me about yesterday."

"It's a free country. You have no right to tell me where I can and can't go." She looked at Lydia again, her expression cold. "Be careful about this one. In case you can't tell, he's still fixated on me, and so controlling too."

"I don't have time for this. We have to go," Jude snapped.

Lydia very much did not want to get involved, so she just clicked her tongue at Saffron, who seemed confused about why she wasn't allowed to say hi to a person she knew, and they set off down the trail, giving Madison a wide berth. Her lips were pressed together as she watched them go, and when Lydia glanced back just before they rounded the curve at the bottom of the hill, she saw Madison still standing there, watching them.

"I'm sorry about that," Jude said gruffly once they were back in the parking lot. "I have no idea how she found us."

"Do you have any idea what she wants?" Lydia asked.

He took his keys out of his pocket to unlock his truck and reached inside for a towel to dry off Saffron's feet.

"I have no idea. I hope she doesn't think she has a chance of getting back into my good graces, because it's not going to happen. I know you have nothing but my word to go on, but please be cautious of her. Even if Derek is the one behind the murder and the vandalism, I still think she could be dangerous."

"I trust you over her any day," Lydia assured him. She lifted up each of Safran's feet for him to wipe off, then patted the seat to tell the dog to jump up into the cab, where Saffron took her place in the middle of the bench seat. "I'm more concerned about how she found us today. Should she have known to look for you here?"

He shook his head. "I didn't discover this place until after I broke things off with her. She shouldn't have known we would be here. I hope it was just a coincidence, because otherwise, it means she's back to her old habits. And that's the last thing I want to deal with."

ELEVEN

Jude dropped her and Saffron off at home before going to the police station to meet with the arresting officer and hopefully get to the bottom of the escalating string of bad luck he had experienced over the past week.

Even though Lydia hoped it really was as simple as an angry poacher seeking revenge on the man who arrested him, her gut told her it wasn't that easy. Derek's grudge didn't explain why Caleb had been in Jude's house, or why his safe was stolen. Whoever killed Caleb seemed to have known that the safe was in his bedroom closet, and Derek the poacher wouldn't have known that. He also wouldn't have had any reason to key Lydia's SUV, though that could have been unconnected.

When Jude got back to her house that afternoon, he looked frustrated.

"He won't admit to anything," he told her. "He's claiming that the blood he had in his vehicle was pig's blood he picked up from a butcher, and he had the receipt to back it up. He said he was on his way home to make blood sausage when he realized he had taken the wrong turn and needed to use my driveway to turn around. Even though he has a motive and he doesn't have an alibi for any of the other incidents, they aren't able to hold him without evidence or a confession."

"That's not fair," she said, aghast. "He was in your driveway with a bucket full of *blood* less than a week after someone *murdered* a man there. That should be enough for them to get a search warrant or charge him with something."

"Trust me, I'm frustrated as well," he said. "On the bright side, Detective Bronner was there, and he confirmed my house will be back in my possession on Monday, though he suggested I hire a professional cleaning company before moving back in."

"You're welcome to stay on my couch for as long as you need," she assured him. "Honestly, if they're releasing Derek and we still don't know who's behind all of this, you're probably safer staying here."

"That might be true, but if someone is out to get me and they find out I'm staying here, then you might be in danger too."

"I think we've been pretty careful so far. Plus, I hate the thought of Saffron being alone in your house while you work all day if someone's after you."

He looked at his dog, who was lying happily on a bed made of folded blankets and chewing on one of her toys, and grimaced. "That's a good point. Assuming this isn't over by the time I go back home, would you mind if I dropped her off here during the day? I hate to use you as a glorified dog sitter, but I can't stand the thought of someone hurting her to get to me."

"Of course," she assured him. "I don't want anything to happen to her either, and I enjoy having her around. You're welcome to drop her off here whenever you want."

Even though nothing had really changed, they remained on edge for the rest of the weekend. Derek's release and Madison ambushing them on the trail had both been an unpleasant reminder that all they were doing was waiting for the next disaster to strike. She wished she knew more about Madison and what exactly she was capable of, but she didn't want to make the whole situation even more stressful for Jude by grilling him about his ex.

Things came to a head on Sunday evening, when she was closing the living room curtains for the night and spotted a silver SUV parked across the street and a little way down the block. She knew silver SUVs weren't exactly rare, but her gut told her it was Madison's, and her blood turned to ice in her veins. She yanked the curtains shut and hurried to find Jude, dragging him over to the window to peer around the edges of the curtain, but by then, the SUV was gone.

Still, she was certain of what she had seen. "She knows you're staying here. I'm sure it was her. She must have seen me at the window and realized I saw her."

"In that case, it's time for me to go home," he told her. "I have more personal days I can take off. Forget the cleaner, I'll handle it myself. My being here is putting you at risk, and I can't let that happen. I don't want to bring Saffron back until the house is clean, though, so would you mind me leaving her here for another day or two?"

She shook her head. "I'm not kicking you out, Jude —"

"The last thing I want is for you to get hurt because of something that has to do with me," he said, interrupting her. He reached out and squeezed her shoulder, letting his hand linger. "You've already done more than enough to help me. I've had a wonderful time staying with you, but I can't hide out here forever, and I can't put you at risk. I'll be careful; I'll change the locks, and I'll get a security camera so I can check on the place while I'm gone. If she so much as steps foot on my property, I'll swing by the station with proof and see what my options are."

"You shouldn't go back there alone."

"I'll give Daniel a call and see if he can take tomorrow morning off to help me get things tidied up and change the locks."

She could tell he wasn't going to be swayed from his decision, and it was true that he would have to go back home eventually. That didn't mean she was going to wash her hands of the whole thing, though. If she could figure out how Madison kept tracking them down, then maybe she could do something to stop it.

TWELVE

Jude left after breakfast on Monday morning to get started on cleaning up his house. Lydia had the evening shift at the restaurant, which meant she had a lot of time to kill. She decided to do what she had been putting off all weekend and type up her plan for an advertising campaign that would actually help improve Iron and Flame's profits without putting their budget in the red.

She spent two hours on her laptop in the living room with Saffron curled up next to her on the couch, doing research about online advertisement campaigns and the best-reviewed marketing professionals that they could contact for a quote. After typing everything up and printing out the pages, she stapled them together and went into the kitchen to set them on the counter under her purse, ensuring that she wouldn't forget them on her way to work that afternoon.

With a little luck, Jeremy would like her plan, and everyone would be happy, solving her problems at the restaurant, if not in the rest of her life.

A glance at the clock over the stove told her it wasn't even noon yet. She texted Jude, who replied with an assurance that everything was all right, and that Daniel was there helping him out. She wandered back into the living room, looking out the window, half expecting to see a silver SUV parked across the street again, but there was nothing there.

She wished she knew what to expect from Madison. It sounded like she didn't have a job, so what did she spend all day doing? Was she driving around town looking for Jude right now? She would probably expect him to be at work, so maybe he would be safe until this evening. Or maybe she was at the restaurant, looking for Lydia's vehicle so she could take a key to the paint again.

"Why does life have to be so stressful?" she muttered to Saffron, who wagged her tail in response. When

Lydia got up, she had sprawled out on her back on the couch and didn't look like she was planning on moving anytime soon. The dog certainly wasn't suffering from any of this.

If Lydia wanted to learn more about Madison, pacing around her house wasn't going to get her anywhere. She needed to talk to someone who actually *knew* Madison. Jude would be ideal, but he was busy right now, and he had enough on his mind as it was.

But maybe a mutual friend of his and Madison's could help. She knew that Alicia had stayed in touch with Madison over the years, despite seeming to disapprove of the other woman's behavior. She didn't have Alicia's phone number, but she knew the other woman worked at the library. It couldn't hurt to stop in, ask if Alicia minded if she gave her a call after work, and maybe check out a book to read. Without Jude staying here this week, the house was going to feel a lot emptier, and she was going to need something to keep her occupied.

After letting Saffron outside one last time, she headed out to her SUV, pausing to triple-check that her front door was locked. She didn't like knowing that Madison was out there somewhere, and that she knew where Lydia lived.

The library was in the historical part of town, near the courthouse. It was an old, two-story brick building, with an activity center on the first level and the books on the second level. She parked in the small parking lot and went inside, climbing the creaky stairs up to the second floor.

The library wasn't very busy; she saw only one other patron sitting at one of the small, round tables, typing on their laptop. She looked over at the service counter and was relieved to see Alicia behind the counter, fiddling with an old printer.

She decided to talk to her before looking for books and made her way over to the counter instead of heading toward the shelves. Alicia looked up as she approached and smiled at Lydia in recognition.

"Oh, hey. Fancy seeing you here. You wouldn't happen to know anything about printers, would you?"

She kept her voice low, so as not to disturb the single patron, and Lydia did the same when she responded. "Unfortunately, I don't. Whenever mine stops working, I just unplug it and then plug it back in. Sometimes it takes a few tries, but it usually works eventually."

"This one keep saying there's no paper in the tray, but I can assure you, there is definitely paper in the tray." She gave up with a sigh. "I'll leave a note and hope someone else can figure it out. What can I help you with? Are you looking for something in particular?"

"Actually, I was hoping I could get your number. There's something I want to ask you about. Could I call you later this evening?"

"Sure, I'll write it down for you." She grabbed a sticky note and scribbled her number out, then handed it to Lydia and said, "How's Jude doing? Does he know when the police will let him back into his house?"

"He's there today," Lydia said hesitantly. "He said Daniel was helping him clean up."

Alicia frowned. "He is?"

"He didn't tell you?"

"I'm sure he just forgot to mention it." She sighed. "He probably didn't tell me because he knew I would be mad. He had to use up a lot of his personal time at the beginning of the year for some personal reasons. Any time he takes off now is going to come out of his salary, and we've got medical bills to pay, so I've been stressing about money. I know Jude's his friend, though, and I can't blame him for wanting to help. You know what, if you want to chat now, you're welcome to pop into the back room with me. I have to sort through some returns, and that way we won't disturb anyone."

She wasn't sure what to think about Daniel keeping that from his wife, but she wasn't about to turn down the chance to get her questions answered. She followed Alicia into the back room, where Alicia rolled a cart full of books over to a table and started sorting through them.

"So, what do you want to know about Madison? Has she been bothering Jude again?"

"I don't have any proof, but I think she's been following both of us over the past few days. She arranged to run in to me at the restaurant, and I could swear that she was waiting outside the auto shop last week when we picked Jude's truck up. Then, this weekend, she ran into us while we were hiking. I can't figure out how she's doing it. I feel like I'm going crazy."

"You should listen to your gut," Alicia said. "If you think she's following you, she probably is."

"Did she do anything like this last time, when Jude was first having problems with her?"

"Well, she broke into his phone and installed an app to track him right before they broke up," Alicia said. "Could she have done that again?"

"I don't think so. He always has his phone with him, so I don't see how she could have gotten it. And there's nothing else…"

Trailing off, Lydia frowned. What if the tracker wasn't an app she installed, but an actual, physical device? Thinking back, she realized there *was* one common element to all of the incidents where Madison had inexplicably shown up.

Jude's truck. She had been outside the auto shop when they picked it up, and the day she confronted Lydia at the restaurant was the day Lydia had taken the truck to work. Had Madison thought Jude was spending the day at the restaurant with her? They had taken his truck to the trail on Saturday, and when she saw Madison's SUV parked across the road from her house, Jude's truck had been parked in her driveway.

It would have been easy for her to hide a small tracking device somewhere on the underside of the truck or in the bed, somewhere Jude wouldn't notice for a long time, if ever.

"Are you all right? Did you think of something?" Alicia asked.

"I think I know how she's been finding us. If I'm right, that means she knows Jude is at his house right now, instead of at work. I might be on the wrong track, but I need to call him just in case."

"If he answers, tell him I want to talk to Daniel. He's in the doghouse."

Lydia nodded and took out her phone, dialing Jude's number. It rang through to voicemail. She redialed immediately, with the same results.

"He's not picking up."

Alicia frowned. "Here, let me try Daniel."

She handed her phone over to Alicia so the other woman could type her husband's number in. Putting it on speakerphone, she hit the button to call him.

The call rang and rang, and finally went to voicemail. Silently, Lydia tried again, then met Alicia's eyes, seeing her concern reflected in them.

"What are the chances that they would *both* have their phones on silent?" Alicia asked. "I'm worried now. I can't get out of here until this afternoon. Can you make sure everything's all right?"

"I'll go right over to Jude's," Lydia said, already moving toward the door. "They should be there. I'll reach out as soon as I know what's going on."

THIRTEEN

Lydia drove to Jude's house as quickly as she dared, the sinking feeling in her stomach only growing stronger as she got closer. She wished they had thought about tracking devices sooner. It seemed like such an extreme action for someone to take. Maybe she was wrong, and Madison just had way too much time on her hands.

She turned onto his street and nearly went dizzy with relief when she saw the two men unloading supplies from the bed of an unfamiliar truck. Jude's truck was parked further up the driveway, so she assumed the second truck was Daniel's. It looked like they had just gotten back from the store. They were alive and well, and just too preoccupied to answer their phones.

Jude looked up as she approached and waved at her. She waved back, then slowed down to park along the curb across the street from his house, since there wasn't room in the driveway. She undid her seatbelt and grabbed her purse before opening her car door and stepping out onto the street. Alicia would be relieved too, though Lydia suspected she was still going to be irritated that Daniel hadn't told her he was taking more time off from work. She felt a little silly for overreacting, but at least she knew Jude was all right.

She took her phone out of her purse and started typing a message to Alicia.

"Watch out!"

She looked up at Jude's shout just in time to see the silver SUV that was racing toward her. She jumped back reflexively, but it wasn't a graceful motion. She tripped over her feet and went down backward, the back of her head colliding with her SUV's side mirror hard enough to make her see nothing but a starburst for a moment.

The silver SUV clipped the front of her vehicle and then careened into a streetlight, where it finally came to a stop. The engine died in a rush of steam and the ping of rapidly cooling metal.

"Lydia!" Jude shouted.

He rushed across the street to her. Just as he reached her, the silver SUV's driver's side door opened, and Madison stumbled out. She wavered for a moment, then spotted Lydia and stomped over to her, shoving Jude out of the way before aiming a vicious kick at Lydia's leg. Lydia grunted and pulled her leg back, raising her arms just in time to block the second kick, which was aimed at her face.

Someone dragged Madison back, and then Jude was there, helping Lydia to her feet. She looked over to see Daniel holding Madison's arms behind her back, his face flushed with anger as he shouted at her.

"You almost killed her!"

"Are you all right?" Jude asked Lydia, checking her over.

"I hit my head, and she kicked me pretty hard, but I'll live ... I think."

She stared at Madison, utterly stunned that the woman had just tried to kill her. Jude had warned her that he thought she was dangerous, but she hadn't expected her to do something like *this*.

"What were you thinking?" Daniel snapped at Madison. "This was attempted murder!"

"I was bringing Jude flowers and lunch," Madison said. She had tears in her eyes, but Lydia suspected they were crocodile tears. "I thought we could make up. I didn't mean to hit her. She was looking down at her phone. She didn't see me coming. It's not my fault."

"Bull," Jude said. "Your SUV swerved *toward* her. How did you even know I was here?"

"I think she's been tracking your truck," Lydia told him.

Madison gave her a nasty look. Daniel frowned. "Jude, can you go get the zip ties out of my truck? I'll secure her, then we'll see if Lydia is right."

Jude nodded and put an arm around Lydia's waist so she could lean against him as he led her over to Daniel's truck. He had her lean against the vehicle before he opened the door and rummaged around for the zip ties. Daniel forcibly manhandled Madison over, and between the two of them, they bound her wrists behind her back.

Daniel convinced her to sit in the passenger seat and made a show of pocketing the keys so even if she got the zip ties off, she couldn't go anywhere. Then he went up the hill to Jude's truck and started searching it inch by inch.

While Daniel looked for the tracking device, Jude examined the bruise that was just blooming on her arm and gently touched the back of her head. "We need to get you to the hospital. Head wounds are serious."

Lydia thought she might be in shock. She felt numb, and her hands were shaking even though she didn't feel cold. "I can't believe she almost killed me."

"Found it!" Daniel called out.

He held up a small square device and jogged back down the hill to them. "It was taped up under your bed cover. It's the type that pings off of the closest phone, so she would have been able to track it almost anywhere."

Jude paled. "I want to ask her some questions."

All three of them went over to the passenger side of Daniel's truck and Daniel opened the door. Madison glared out at them.

"How long were you following me?" Jude asked, his voice tight with anger.

"Long enough to know things aren't serious between you and her. I want to get back together with you, Jude. We never should have broken up. You don't want to be with someone like her, do you?"

"Madison, even if I hadn't just witnessed you attempt to *murder* someone I care about, I would never have agreed to having you be a part of my life again. Do you not realize what you put me through after we broke up? On top of that, you were unfaithful to me during our relationship. It's over, and it's been over between us for a long time. I don't understand why you're doing all of this *now*."

She sniffed, tears coming to her eyes again. "Hugh left me with nothing. I've been living in my vehicle, couch hopping, and begging my friends to let me use their showers and buy me lunch. I deserve to live comfortably. Just let me move in with you, give me a little bit of money every month, and I'll be the perfect girlfriend. I know you can afford to give me the sort of life I deserve, Jude."

He gave a disbelieving laugh. "I'm a game warden, making the same salary as I was making two years ago. Why do you suddenly think I'm rich?"

"I heard about your grandmother's passing," Madison said. "I know she left you a lot of money. You're not going to do anything with it on your own. I can help you put it to good use."

He stared at her, befuddled. "She didn't have any money, Madison. She was on round-the-clock care for the last few years of her life. She spent it all."

She stared at him for a long moment, her expression slowly contorting into a look of rage. She looked mad enough to kill.

Lydia finally put it together.

"You thought he was rich," she said, staring at Madison. "And I bet you knew he had a safe hidden in his closet where he kept all his important documents." She looked at Jude. "The break-in happened a few days after you got back from your grandmother's will reading. That wasn't a coincidence."

His eyes widened. "She took the safe to look for money or bank account information, maybe even a check. She thought my grandmother left me a small fortune."

Daniel crossed his arms. "What am I missing?"

Jude looked at Madison like he had never really seen her before. "I'm saying I think she's the one who broke into my house and stole my safe. Which must mean she's the one who killed Caleb."

Madison gave Jude a look of innocence that was so fake, it was almost laughable. "Caleb? What happened to Caleb?"

Daniel shot her a dark look. "I know for a fact that Alicia called you to tell you about his death. Don't try that on us. What really happened?"

Madison's face twisted. "Fine, you want the truth? It was all Caleb's idea. I was staying at his place when he learned about Jude's grandmother dying. I mentioned in passing that she was rich. That Monday, when he asked you how the will reading had gone, you told him you just put everything in your safe and you were going to look at it later. Caleb thought it was the perfect chance for us both to get a little bit of breathing room, financially speaking. The tracker was his idea; I put it in your truck so we could know for sure when you were gone."

"Did you put water in the gas tank, too? And spread the trash around my yard?"

"What?" She made a face. "No. What are you talking about?"

The vandalism must have been Derek, Lydia realized. It was just bad luck that he started it at the same time Madison and Caleb put their plan into action. It had thrown both them and the police off.

"How did Caleb end up dead?" Daniel asked, his expression hard. Caleb had been his friend too, Lydia remembered.

She hesitated, but Lydia could see the moment she realized that she was in too deep to back out now.

"We got the safe into the living room when he started getting cold feet. He thought maybe we should put it back, that it wasn't fair to you. He said you'd been a good friend, and you didn't deserve this. I *needed* that money. I wasn't about to let him wreck things for me. When he bent down to pick up the safe and take it back to your bedroom, I saw one of those dumb bells on the floor and I did what I had to do. A woman's got to look out for herself."

She looked down at them, her expression arrogant, but it slowly turned uncertain as the reality of her situation started to sink in.

"What are you going to do to me? I was desperate. I needed the money to live. I shouldn't be punished for that. It isn't fair."

"You want fair?" Daniel asked. "It doesn't get much fairer than an impartial court of law."

She started to cry—for real this time, Lydia thought —but Daniel shut the truck's door, effectively silencing her as he turned to Jude. "I'll take her in. You take care of Lydia."

Jude nodded his thanks and led Lydia toward his truck. "I'll take you to the hospital," he said. "Daniel will take care of everything else. I'm so sorry, Lydia. I had no idea that she would do something like this. I never wanted to put you in danger."

"Well, there is one silver lining," Lydia murmured. Jude looked down at her, confused. She gave him a weak smile. "When you meet Jeremy, he's going to seem like an absolute peach compared to her."

EPILOGUE

Come to Iron and Flame for our lunch special Monday through Friday, and leave feeling like part of the family!

The short video ended with a group shot of herself, Jeremy, and all of their employees—even Hank, though the elderly, part-time chef had grumbled and complained the whole time he was there—gathered in the restaurant's kitchen together.

All of their smiles, even Hank's, were genuine, and Lydia thought that came through in the photo. The ad was now running on every major website they had been able to purchase a slot for, and they were already beginning to see an uptick in business during the week.

It was a little odd to see an advertisement for her own restaurant while she was trying to watch a video review of the dog bed she wanted to buy for Saffron, but she thought she could get used to it. She knew she wasn't the only member of the staff who kept seeing the video when they got online, because her employees kept cheering whenever one of them spotted it.

She had to admit that Jeremy's idea for an advertisement had been a good one, with just a little tweaking. Communication had never been their strong suit, but they had gotten there in the end, as they always did.

At least with Jude, every other discussion didn't lead to an argument. Though stressful, the events that had culminated in Madison's arrest had brought them closer together. They had handled it as a team, and she thought they made a very good team.

They made good friends, too, and she was becoming more and more certain she wanted more. It could wait, though. They had been through a lot, and some time to relax and let their lives get back to normal would be nice. With a little luck, the next few months would be drama free, and she could enjoy the spring weather and the restaurant's success without any worries.

Printed in Great Britain
by Amazon